The Halfling

Nikki Moyes

Author: Moyes, Nikki

Publisher: Moyes Publishing

Title: **The Halfling**/Nikki Moyes.

ISBN: 9780648514954

For all the halflings.
The blood of the covenant is thicker
than the water of the womb.

Bronzrr

"Once upon a time, we dragons lived peacefully among the humans, until one day a man called Mellakai attacked our clan. Three dragons were injured that day and the war between our people began."

"Why did he do it, Bron?"

I glanced away from the crystal-clear lake to glare at Sapphia. She sat in human-form, cross-legged on the ground with her fair hair hanging loose around the shoulders of the dress her mother had woven from local vines. The little hatchling stared intently up at me with big, brown human eyes.

"He was a bad man." I glanced back to the peaceful lake.

"Why was he a bad man?"

"He just was." My reflection stared back at me; smooth masculine body of my dragon-rider guise, dark hair and green dragon eyes.

"Was he born bad?"

"Yes, he was born bad," I replied.

"How was he born bad?"

"He just was." I blew out a breath of annoyance at being dragged into another debate with the five-year-old hatchling.

"Maybe he wasn't bad. Maybe he was born wrong, like me," Sapphia said.

"Who said you were born wrong?" I demanded, turning to look at her.

"Grandpa Rubyss." She looked at me as though I held her heart and the answers to the universe.

I attempted to maintain a neutral expression. I couldn't disagree with anything our elder said. Yet my little Sapphia, the one who would have become my mate for life if she wasn't half-human, was nothing like the monster Mellakai the Dragon Hunter.

"Some people are just not nice," I said, before it occurred to me I wasn't clear whether I was talking about Mellakai or her grandfather, Elder Rubyss.

"But..."

"Do you want me to finish the story, or not?" I continued before she interrupted again. "Mellakai paid a witch to create a deadly twin-pronged sword–"

"Was the witch bad?"

"Sapphia..." I growled.

She clamped her hands over her mouth and stared up at me with those wide, innocent eyes.

"The sword had a jewelled handle and poisonous green edge, with a tip that could flex to slide up under scales and pierce our hearts. He called it Slayer."

I gave a jabbing motion with my arm and she gasped. Sapphia was easy to scare.

"Mellakai murdered many of our clan over the following years and with each death the victim's name was seared across the blade. Mellakai was injured multiple times, but would not die. Some believe he drank the blood of the slain to absorb our powers."

Sapphia leaned forward, her eyes wide.

"In the end, to save our clan, we departed that world, leaving behind a single dragon to protect our temple to the elders, Aurum and his mate Argentum. The Temple Keeper's name was Dargren. He took dragon-rider form to protect his true identity from Mellakai's people. So, little hatchlings like you need to behave or Mellakai's spirit will come after you." I added that bit to tease her.

Sapphia trailed her fingers across the golden sand. "What happened to Slayer?"

I had no idea. It wasn't even the point of the story. It was about doing as you were told or the bad man would get you.

"I imagine it's been destroyed. It was a long time ago," I said.

"But what if Mellakai had a child, who had a child, who had a child..."

"Humans breed indiscriminately. I get the point," I interrupted.

"But what if the sword was passed down through the hunter's family and someone still has it?" She looked up at me with those big trusting eyes.

The hairs on my arms rose and the feeling of my scales trying to burst to the surface crept over me. We had no idea where Slayer was. The story was meant to scare Sapphia, not me.

Before I could form a knowledgeable answer, Sapphia tensed and glanced over her shoulder. I narrowed my eyes and searched the sky until I could pick out what she had sensed. In the distance, several dragons glided towards the lake.

It was not worth my reputation to be seen speaking to the halfling, especially standing there in human-form. I did what I did best – illusions. I disappeared from sight. When Sapphia turned back, she couldn't see me.

She stumbled to her feet and wrapped her arms around her small human body. She glanced around the sandy beach by her favourite swimming place, searching for somewhere to hide, but there was nowhere she could reach without being seen. She started to run.

Our clan-mates swooped towards us and Sapphia switched into her scales. No one could change form as fast as Sapphia. It was instantaneous and the newcomers roared. A half-human shouldn't be more dragon than we were.

Sapphia flapped her leathery wings frantically, but she was too young to achieve ground take-off. The teenage dragons landed in a circle surrounding her. She cowered before them, pressing her body into the sand.

"Worthless half-breed," Assh hissed.

"Nobody wants you here. You stink of human," Ssienna added. My fingers curled into my palms.

"Leave me alone." Sapphia's voice broke as tears fell down her scaly cheeks.

"Who's going to make us?" They laughed.

She searched the group and for a moment I was gripped by a fear that she'd say my name and I'd have to choose between her and my future.

"Ammee will punish you." Sapphia used her mother's shortened name instead of mine.

I took a tentative step sideways, judging if I could fetch Amethyss without being noticed, when Viridiss flicked her tail at the hatchling. Sapphia was sent flying, hitting a small boulder with a yelp.

I made a move forward before remembering I needed to stay out of this if I was going to earn a position in Elder Rubyss' court. The alternative was to become an outcast like Sapphia and her mother.

Sapphia switched to human-form and crawled backwards until her feet dipped into the lake. Viridiss, Assh, and Ssienna crowded around her, forcing her into the lake before taking to the sky to dive bomb her.

Sapphia dived and disappeared into the depths of the water. The others circled above waiting for her until I was afraid she would drown if she didn't come up for air. I wasn't sure how long humans could stay underwater.

I mimicked the sound of the adults' call from our village. Assh cocked his head at the sound.

"Come on, let's go." He took flight and the girls followed. Viridiss was the last to leave, hovering by the water a moment longer, but Sapphia hadn't surfaced. Viridiss leapt into the air after our hatch-mates.

I broke my invisibility illusion and ran to the water's edge ready to dive in, but Sapphia's blonde head emerged before I could. She splashed feebly towards me. I waded over to fish her out, soaking my trousers in the process. She flopped to the ground, gasping and clutching her side where a patch of red stained her dress.

Her human-form was so fragile with her wet hair covering her face. A smear of blood stained the large rock nearby and a shiny, blue scale lay next to it. I couldn't pick her up in my claws and fly without injuring her further so I was forced to stay in rider form and pick her up in my arms.

"Where did you go, Bron?" she asked as I cradled her against my bare chest. She squeezed her eyes closed and whimpered. I had no answer to give her so I stayed silent.

Amethyss and Sapphia's home cave sat a long way up the side of a cliff away from the main clan caves. My dragon-rider form wasn't capable of scaling the rocks with Sapphia in my arms.

A shiver rolled over me. The journey would require me to step out of existence. I closed my eyes, visualised the entrance to the cave, sucked in a breath, and stepped out of existence.

For a fraction of a moment, all of my senses were lost. I tighten my grip on Sapphia in case I lost her while I couldn't feel touch. Then my senses returned and I stood at the entrance of the cave with Sapphia crying out from my tightened hold.

Amethyss lumbered over as soon as she saw us. I avoided her twitching tail as I lay her injured daughter on a bed of grasses. She nuzzled Sapphia anxiously as she inspected the wound. With her claws, she tore away the dress from Sapphia's side and I glanced away as Sapphia cried out in pain.

"Is there anything I can do?" I found myself asking.

"No, Bronzrr. The injury is minor. My energy will heal her. You should go before my father hears you were here.

It would ruin your chances of becoming the next Story Keeper."

"What if I don't want the responsibility of keeping all of the clan's stories?" I clasped my hands behind my back.

"You have a talent for the stories. Don't waste it. Sapphia has her own destiny," Amethyss replied. She turned her back on me, halting any questions I had about what she knew of Sapphia's future.

I glanced at Sapphia lying there with only her mother for comfort and pain formed in my chest. I visualised the stuffed toy sabre-horn tiger my mother gave me as a child many rotations ago. No one had ever seen a real sabre-horn tiger. The felines refused to join our clan when we left our world millennia ago. It was common belief they had died out.

The soft tiger appeared in my hands. The fur was tattered from years of use and one horn hung loose, but I was nearly an adult and too old for toys. For a moment I considered keeping it for memory's sake, but Sapphia needed it more than I did.

I stepped forward to place it in Sapphia's hands. She clutched it to her chest and looked at me as though I'd slain a thousand dragon hunters for her. I didn't want her to look at me like that. I left her in the care of her mother as I switched form and took flight.

The rains began a moon-cycle later. I pitied the land-dwelling creatures below on the planet's surface as I twisted and turned in the sun, sending flashes of bronze dancing off my scales. The clouds below me were so thick I felt like I could fold up my wings and walk across the dense carpet they made. I shook those foolish hatchling thoughts from my mind. It was the sort of childish comment Sapphia would make.

I dived into the clouds for a moment, losing myself completely in the chilly dampness. A brief flash of blue was all the warning I had before something latched onto my tail.

"Found you! I'm practicing my flying!" Sapphia yelled gleefully as I flicked my tail from her jaws.

I turned my head to snap at the tiny ball of sapphire who had somehow learned to fly long before any other hatchling. I kept one eye on her as I rolled to my right. There was no hint of her half-breed genes beneath her shiny sapphire scales. Sapphia beat her tiny wings rapidly to catch up with me, the stuffed toy tiger clutched in her talons.

"I can't play with you anymore," I said.

She bobbed her head up and down. "Ammee says you're going to be the next Story Keeper."

"Only if Elder Rubyss doesn't catch me hanging around a half-breed," I muttered under my breath.

I tried to lose her in the dense clouds, but it was as if she could sense my presence. Even my larger wings were ineffective. She caught up to me eventually, looking puffed and pleased with herself.

"I have a story for you." Sapphia sucked air into her lungs as she rested on an air current. "I know where Slayer is."

"Don't make up tales, Sapphia." I glided for a moment.

"I'm not. Ammee has seen a human with it." Sapphia darted in front of me.

I flapped my wings, soaring out of the cool clouds and back into the bright sunshine. I twisted as I rose, sending flashes of blinding light dancing across the clouds. Sapphia whistled in pleasure as if I'd put on the display solely for her. I turned and growled at her and for a moment she flinched at my aggression.

"Don't you want to know about Slayer?"

"Leave me alone, Sapphia. Go find your mother."

"Ammee's busy. She said she had to speak to someone about a contract and I should go play on my own. What's a contract, Bron?"

"It's adult business."

I folded my wings and plummeted towards the surface of the planet. Today I would not worry about whether she made it home safely. She had made it up here, she could find her own way home. I couldn't be her hatchling-sitter.

The rain had morphed into a fine drizzle by the time I landed on the ledge of my new cave. Sapphia's uncle Ambress waited inside, crouched on the stone floor as though he might strike at any moment. I hesitated at the entrance and lowered my body to the floor in a submissive pose.

"Rubyss wants to know how you're progressing with Ssyan?" Ambress stalked towards me. "I said you were too young to learn our stories by rote, but old Ssyan insists on training you. He says you have the heart of a storyteller."

"The Story Keeper has me working hard. I've already memorised the first three stories and I'm on my way to see him now." I stayed low.

"You won't allow the half-breed to corrupt your education?"

"No, sire." I kept my eyes averted.

"I can smell her scent on you." Ambress pushed his snout towards me.

"I saw Sapphia earlier, but I told her to leave me alone."

"Good. My sister may have brought shame on our clan by hatching a human child, but I won't allow our history to be put at risk."

Fine tendrils of smoke rose from Ambress' nostrils. He lumbered past me and with a single sweep of his amber wings, he took to the skies. I rose from my prostrated position and watched his departure.

I turned in a few circles and studied the grey sky again. Ambress had disappeared and there was no sign of Sapphia. I snorted out a small cloak of smoke and took to the sky.

Old Ssyan lounged in his cave when I arrived. My eyes followed the Story Keeper medallion hanging around his neck. The carved dragon held centre position surrounded by other creatures of myth. Ssyan had allowed me to touch the medallion for a moment during my coming-of-age ceremony. My paws tingled at the memory of the power flowing through it. One day it would be mine to guard.

"What shall you learn today, young one?" Ssyan's voice was gravelly with age.

"What happened to Slayer?" I asked.

Ssyan narrowed one beady eye on me. "Why do you ask?"

"I heard that Amethyss may have seen it when she was away from our clan six years ago." I shifted nervously on my paws.

"Do not believe the tales she tells," Ssyan hissed. "Amethyss believes herself to hold our secret stories. She dishonours me and the males of our clan. She shames us with her half-human hatchling, claiming it's the will of Argentum."

"If I'm to be the Story Keeper when you pass to the Otherside, shouldn't I know of the untrue stories also?" I dared to ask.

Ssyan snorted and eyed me for a long moment before responding.

"Amethyss came to me the day after her grandmother, Magentass, passed to the Otherside. She said she'd been entrusted with one of Argentum's stories."

"But the stories belong to Aurum, not his mate." I frowned.

"I see you've been listening." Ssyan bobbed his head up and down. "'Tell me this story,' I said to Amethyss, although

I knew Aurum never entrusted his female with one of our precious stories."

Ssyan stared off into the distance and I stayed silent waiting for him to continue.

"'The daughters of Argentum have been tasked with ensuring their children are genetically the best in existence,' Amethyss said to me. 'You are the descendant of the Elders Aurum and Argentum', I replied. 'You can't get more perfect than that.'

"She looked at me then and spoke the words I can never unhear – 'Grandmother Magentass believed we are no longer the superior race.'"

I gasped and stared at the old dragon. Ssyan turned in a quick circle and settled on the floor again, before continuing.

"'If not us, then who?' I demanded of Amethyss. She stared me in the eye like she was Rubyss himself and replied, 'Mellakai's descendants'. I looked at her with derision, but she continued anyway. 'I went back to our old home to see if Grandmother was right,' Amethyss said. 'And I saw humans with dragon's blood flowing through their veins, the children of the hunter, Mellakai'.

"She paused and stared off into the distance, but I didn't dare disturb her delusion." Ssyan's tongue flicked out, tasting the air.

"'I saw a single man face down a rebellion attempting to destroy humans who could shift their form into animals, just as we can take on rider form,' she said. 'There is no dragon alive who holds that kind of power. Surely it is my duty to obey the will of Argentum?'

"I stared at Amethyss for a long moment before responding," Ssyan continued. "'It is your duty to honour your clan,' I replied after enough time to appear to have considered her question seriously. 'There are so few mating dragons left that you must join with whomever your father chooses.'

"She nodded her head as though listening to my advice, but several days later she was gone. When she eventually returned to us, she had the half-breed child with her."

"So Amethyss didn't betray our clan? Sapphia is the will of Argentum?" My tail swept the floor.

"No!" Ssyan surged towards me with speed unexpected from a dragon of his centuries. I flinched and he stopped a scale-width from my face.

"Amethyss is delusional. She made up the story. The only true stories are Aurum's. A Story Keeper cannot associate himself with the likes of Amethyss and Sapphia. Now leave me be, fledgling. I will tell you a new tale tomorrow." Ssyan lumbered off to the depths of his cave and I slunk away.

Dusk fell as I flew home. I detoured via Amethyss' cave, rehearsing the words I would say to Sapphia when I told her I couldn't be seen with her anymore.

Their cave was empty. I sniffed the still air, but no one had been here all day. Smoke rose into my checks. Sapphia found me this morning, she could find her way home again. She must be with Amethyss somewhere. I'd tell her later.

I took flight again. As I landed on my cave stoop, Viridiss dropped out of the sky and landed beside me.

"What do you want?" I demanded.

"The halfling was looking for you this morning," she said.

My hackles rose. "So?"

"It wouldn't be fitting for the Story Keeper-in-training to be seen with a half-human, would it?"

Smoke escaped from my nostrils. "I hardly have time to be spending with Sapphia," I growled.

"You and I could be friends, Bronzrr. Neither one of us have mates after all." Viridiss snaked her murky green tail towards mine, her scales dull compared to Sapphia's brilliance. I shifted out of her reach.

"I hardly think I'll have the time now I'm Story Keeper-in-training. Stay safe in the dark," I bid her farewell and disappeared into my cave. After a few moments, her claws sounded on the rock as she took flight. I sighed and curled up in my nest.

A faint noise by the cave entrance woke me from sleep hours later. I kept my eyes closed, but Sapphia crept closer and nudged me with her head. Underneath her usual scent of fresh charcoal and violets, was a stench of something charred.

I opened an eye and took in her drooping wings and bowed head. She took a deep breath.

"She's gone," Sapphia wailed.

I looked her over. She had something sooty clasped in her right fore-talons, but her toy Sabre Horn Tiger was missing. I sighed.

"I can't help you anymore, Sapphia. Go back to your family."

"Ambress says half-breeds don't have family and that includes uncles," she sobbed.

I tensed and flames licked the back of my throat. I wished I had the nerve to stand up to Ambress for Sapphia. I snuffed out the flame when panic crossed her face as she misunderstood my reaction. She stumbled backwards.

"Uncle Ambress won't find me here," she blurted out. "He's arguing with Grandpa Rubyss..."

"Did you make them mad again, Sapphia?"

"I didn't mean to. I need help..."

"Go back to your mother, Sapphia. I'm training to be the next Story Keeper. Ssyan will find someone else if you keep hanging around here. We can't be friends any longer."

"You don't love me anymore?" she whispered.

"I don't love you, Sapphia." I swallowed around the lump forming in the back of my throat. Another tear rolled down her cheek.

"I hate you." Tentacles of smoke drifted from her nostrils and mingled with tears. She wasn't big enough to breathe fire yet.

She stepped backwards and tried to take off, but tripped and fell to the ground below. I hovered near the edge of my cave, but I couldn't check on her. It would ruin all the work I put into looking like I didn't care.

Her sobs reached me and my chest tightened. I closed my eyes and pictured the Story Keeper medallion. It would be mine one day. A dragon with no royal blood would become one of the most trusted males in Rubyss' court. Without it, I'd never amount to anything.

Sapphia

"I hate you." The words slipped out and mingled with my smoky tears.

I stumbled backwards out of Bron's cave and attempted to take off, but my tired wings folded. I fell off the ledge and crashed into the trees below in a flutter of blue leather and scales. I hit the ground covered in scratches with a torn wing membrane. I lay still for a moment, waiting for Bron to check on me, but he didn't.

The tears began again. I was scared; more terrified than I'd ever been in my whole life. I wanted Ammee to wrap me in her wings and tell me everything was okay, but that wouldn't happen because she was — images flooded my mind.

I'd followed Ammee to a place outside this world. I didn't really know how we got there, but I'd found her taking a book from a library. God-like people stormed into the room and I hid behind a chair. One of the gods struck Ammee with energy and there was smoke and a bad smell and then all her beautiful scales were melted onto the floor of that bad place.

I gasped for air through my tears and shut out the memory of the last few hours. I stumbled into the forest still clutching the single sooty amethyst tail scale in my talons.

That night I huddled under a small rock ledge by the far side of the lake, too scared to return to my home cave alone in case the ones who hurt Ammee had seen me. They could be looking for me right now to make me dead. I reached out to clutch my tiger toy but I must have dropped it. I clung to Ammee's scale and cried myself into a restless sleep.

My dreams were weird and choppy. I was Ammee as a hatchling while her grandmother whispered a story to her about the old dragon elders, Aurum and Argentum.

She whispered of how Aurum and Argentum turned themselves into statues that sat on a crop of rock in the middle of a deep lake to watch over the other dragons and give them guidance.

As I clutched Ammee's scale, tiny bits of her life came to me, things she'd never told me, like meeting my human father, and the location of the world where dragons used to live.

When I woke shortly before dawn, I knew where to go. Aurum and Argentum would know how to get my mummy back. I'd be the first dragon in millennia to see the dragon temple.

I was directed by stories Bron told and strange dream-memories intruding in my mind that didn't belong to me. They began sometime after I lost Amethyss and I didn't know how to stop or even control them.

I could only fly short distances before the pain of my torn wing became unbearable. Instead, I had to step out of existence to reach a new location like I'd done to follow Amethyss to the bad place with the books. It was terrifying on my own. The empty darkness wrapped itself around me. If I panicked, I could be stuck in that nowhere place until I was six or even older.

It was easier the last time because I could think of Ammee to follow her. This time I thought about the dragon temple, but I'd never seen it so it was hard to do.

I stepped back into existence in the sky above the planet where Mellakai the Dragon Hunter once lived. The planet was nearly completely covered in water making it difficult to see where the temple should be.

I glided in a wide circle and for a moment, I could see Dargren's Island glimmering in the ocean some way off the coast of the planet's largest landmass. As I flew towards it, the island vanished like it was never there.

I pulled up abruptly, sending sharp pain through my wing.

I wondered if someone moved the island and didn't tell our clan. Perhaps Dargren hid it so Mellakai couldn't find the island. I don't know if Dargren was the kind of dragon who would hide an island and not tell anyone.

I circled overhead, high above so I looked like a bird in the distance. My wing hurt and humans might still live on the islands. I needed a safe place to rest. A satellite planet orbited this one. It wasn't too far, a short step out of existence and I was there.

I appeared directly above the temple of Aurum and Argentum and dropped out of the sky in shock. It had been moved. I crashed into the lake with a huge splash and hoped there were no humans around to kill me or witness my fall.

Considering my small size and lack of fire-breathing skills, I needed to stay out of sight, unless dragon hunters were afraid of getting a bad cough from my smoke.

I struggled back to the surface of the lake, fighting against the drag of my soaking wings. A rock ledge trapped me beneath the water. Panicking, I forgot how to fission the oxygen from the water like Ammee taught me. As my lungs were about to burst, I surfaced in a dark underground passageway filled with dank air.

I dragged myself from the lake and lay on the smooth stone. After some time, I worked up the energy to shake the water from my wings. I paused when I noticed the glowing images on the walls leading up and away from the water's edge.

Curiosity killed the hatchling, but satisfaction brought her back, that's what Bron always said. I moved closer, my claws tapping quietly on the stone. The pictures looked like a story about the dragons, but without Bron to explain it to me, I didn't know what it meant.

As I walked, I traced my paw over the images while the stone tunnel wound higher above the lake. Near what I hoped was the top of the mountain, large slash marks gouged several of the rock images. My dragon blood boiled at the audacity of whoever caused the damage to our stories. Ammee loved the word 'audacity', especially when talking about her brother Ambress.

For a moment, I considered heading home to tell my elders so that they could hunt down whoever dared damage the temple. Home – I no longer had one. No one wanted me, so it wasn't possible to return.

I tried not to remember. My body trembled. It was how I imagine losing my tail or having my wings torn off, or maybe both at the same time, would feel. It especially hurt to think of Bron. I was missing half of me without him...and he didn't even care.

A tear rolled down my scales as I emerged into the temple beneath the statues of the dragon elders of Aurum and Argentum. I stared up at the canopy created by their outstretched gold and silver wings. Ammee said I was descended from both Aurum and Argentum. That made me special.

The damage in the tunnel continued with a broken crystal sphere near the tunnel entrance. Two whole spheres dotted the open floor space and a glass dome filled with drawings dominated the centre of the temple. Aurum and Argentum's legs, paws and wingtips made up the temple walls. Between the spaces, were glimpses of the lake and surrounding green island.

I marvelled at the feeling of being the first of my clan to see this place. Even Grandpa Rubyss has never dared venture this far from our world. For a moment I was brave and fearless, an explorer finding ancient things without a care in the world.

A movement somewhere near the broken crystal sphere caught my eye. I jumped. Hissing, I raised my wings to appear large and aggressive to whatever lurked there. I didn't know how big dragon hunters were. Hopefully it was smaller than me and wouldn't realise I was only a hatchling.

When whatever it was made no attempt to attack me, I peered closer to get a better look. I gasped. A sabre-horn tiger stared back at me. Judging by the fluffiness of his fur and short horn stumps, this one was young. Much to my relief, he was smaller than me. He was all fluffed up to look bigger than he was, like me. I felt sorry for him being up here all alone without his mother.

Then I got mad at him, because he probably still had a mother waiting for him somewhere, so I hissed at him to make him go away. He cowered behind one of the spheres now trying to look as small and invisible as possible, although he kept peeking at me as if he had never seen a dragon before.

"Who are you?" I demanded.

'Nobody.'

I was momentarily surprised the tiger could mind-speak, but I had a purpose in coming to the temple that didn't involve tiger cubs. I ignored him. Nobody was a stupid name anyway.

'I want my mummy back,' I projected my thoughts to Aurum and Argentum, the temple statues. As a dragon, they should hear my words and respond, even if I was a hatchling – and only half-dragon.

'We cannot do as you ask.' The ancient voices whispered in my head.

I gasped for breath as panic set in. This wasn't how it was meant to happen. I needed Ammee. I didn't know what to do without her and Bron.

'Please,' I begged. *'Don't leave me on my own.'* I sobbed in front of the Great Elders, tears running down my scales.

There was so much pain inside of me. I needed it to stop.

'*Amethyss is dead. She cannot return to you, but you are part of a greater plan for the universe. Your father needs you. We will allow you to forget your past, but you must agree to follow in his footsteps.*'

'*I don't know my father,*' I cried as my body trembled. They wanted me to find a human, on my own.

'*We will tell you where to find him. Think of a name; when you speak it out loud, you will forget. When you hear it again, you will remember.*'

I thought of Ammee. She had a beautiful name to match her bright scales, but I worried my father would speak it. I needed someone who I would never see again, someone who didn't care enough to look for me. I would say his name, the one who should have always been there for me. I turned to the sabre-horn still hiding in the corner.

'Promise me you will never speak this name I am about to say,' I hissed at him.

'Promise,' the little tiger cub thought.

He wasn't my concern anymore. As soon as I spoke the name, everything would go blank. I dropped Ammee's scale on the floor.

"Bronzrr," I said.

About the Author

Nikki Moyes was born in Victoria and moved around Australia amassing an eclectic range of occupations including tall- ship watch leader, apiarist, rose farm hand, and sandwich artist. In her spare time she learns tissu, static trapeze, and aerial hoop (she couldn't decide on one) in case she needs to run off and join the circus.

You can find her here:

www.facebook.com/moyes.nikki/
www.instagram.com/nikkimoyesauthor/
www.goodreads.com/author/show/15606198.Nikki_Moyes

If you enjoyed Bronzrr and Sapphia's story, please leave a review. Their story will continue in THE CHALLENGER – Book 2 of The Suri Series, but first, THE KEEPER – Book 1 of the Suri Series

Other books by Nikki Moyes

The Keeper – Book 1 of the Suri Series

17-year-old Cassie is pressured into a reality dating program, but a contestant is keeping secrets about the mysterious disappearance of the Keeper of the Dragon Temple, and the Governor of the Universe who was born with a thousand years of ancestral memories.

<u>Young Adult Fiction:</u>

If I Wake

The Keeper (Book 1 - Suri Series)

The Castle (Suri Series - short story)

The Halfling (Suri Series - short story)

<u>Fiction:</u>

The Dark Lord's Risk Assessor (short story)

<u>Non-Fiction:</u>

Kokoda Trek: 75th Anniversary

<u>Picture Book:</u>

Let's Imagine What We Will Do